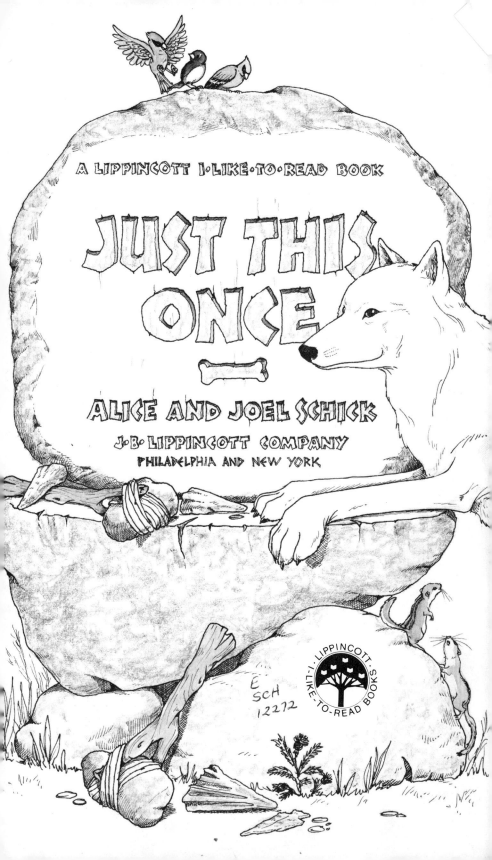

A LIPPINCOTT I·LIKE·TO·READ BOOK

JUST THIS ONCE

ALICE AND JOEL SCHICK

J·B·LIPPINCOTT COMPANY
PHILADELPHIA AND NEW YORK

U.S. Library of Congress Cataloging in Publication Data

Schick, Alice.

Just this once.

(A Lippincott I-like-to-read book)

SUMMARY: Accepting the advances of a lone wolf, a cave family domesticates the first dog.

[1. Dogs—Fiction. 2. Cave dwellers—Fiction] I. Schick, Joel, joint author. II. Title.

PZ7.G3443Ju   [E]   77-28871

ISBN-0-397-31803-0

FOR WILLY
AND IN MEMORY OF
BRANDY AND WINTER

Og and Glok and their children
Tad and Jen lived in a cave high on a
hill.

The other families lived huddled
together at the edge of the lake. They
shook with fear in thunderstorms.
They shivered when wild beasts
howled in the dark forest.

But Og and Glok and Tad and Jen
were not afraid.

10

One day the men were out
mammoth hunting. Along came a
wolf, wagging her tail.

The hunters panicked. They
began to throw spears, sticks and
stones at the wolf. The wolf ran away.
Cursing, the hunters went home.

All except Og. When he was alone, the wolf came back, carrying a stick. She sat in front of Og's feet and wagged her tail.

"All right," said Og. "Just this once." He tossed the stick. The wolf chased it and brought it back.

The game went on so long that Og was late for supper.

14

The gatherers went wild. They screamed and shook their fists until the wolf ran away.

Muttering darkly, the gatherers went home.

The next
gathering r...
Again the w...
her tail.

All except Glok. When she was alone, the wolf came back. She plopped a muddy paw on Glok's hand and said, "Ooo-ooo-ooo-arr-arr-arr."

"All right," said Glok. "Just this once." She scratched the wolf behind the ears. The wolf rolled over for Glok to scratch her belly.

That night, Glok was late for supper.

The next day, Tad watched Rik the
Artist draw a picture on a cave wall.
Along came the wolf once again.

Rik shrieked with terror. His
screams chased the wolf and Tad
away.

When Tad was out of breath he stopped running. The wolf danced around him. Then she stopped, crouched down on her elbows and howled.

"All right," said Tad. "Just this once." He started to run again so the wolf could chase him. Tad and the wolf ran around and around, chasing bugs, birds and each other.

That night, Tad missed supper completely.

The next day, Jen watched Mug the Toolmaker work. The wolf appeared still again.

Mug was horror-struck. He began to make awful noises and throw things. The wolf and Jen ran away.

That night, Jen got home in time
for supper. The wolf came too.

"Can we feed her?" Jen asked.
"Just this once?"

Soon the wolf was practically a member of the family.

The people complained to Bubba the Wise Man, whose word was law.

"The wolf is evil," said the hunters.
"She made us lose a mammoth."

"Because of that beast," said the
gatherers, "we won't have enough
food to last through the winter."

"The wolf ruined my greatest
masterpiece!" yelled Rik the Artist.

"Look what that wolf did to me!"
shouted Mug the Toolmaker, waving
his swollen thumb.

"Hmmm," said Bubba thoughtfully.
"That wolf sounds dangerous. It has
to go. I'll speak to Og and Glok."

But when Bubba stepped inside
the cave, he saw something he hadn't
counted on.

"All right. They can stay," said
Bubba. "Just this once."

And the rest is history.

ALICE and JOEL SCHICK live in a farmhouse in Monterey, Massachusetts, with their son Morgan, six cats, and a dog who looks like a wolf. The Schicks have worked together on several books for children. In addition to *Just This Once,* their books include *Viola Hates Music, The Remarkable Ride of Israel Bissell as Related by Molly the Crow,* and *Serengeti Cats.*

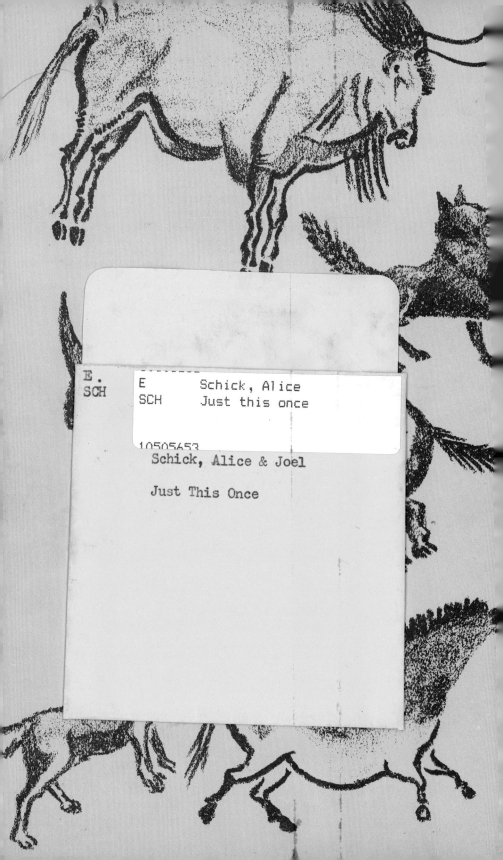

Schick, Alice & Joel

Just This Once